FROGGY PLAYS IN THE BAND

FROGGY PLAYS IN THE BAND

by JONATHAN LONDON
illustrated by FRANK REMKIEWICZ

SCHOLASTIC INC.
New York Toronto London Auckland Sydney
Mexico City New Delhi Hong Kong Buenos Aires

For Emma, Hannah, Leah, Max, D.J., Stephanie, Maia, and Sean—
and for Becky Martin and the Willowside School Band.
    —J. L.

For Froggy's *other* band: Cecilia, Denise, Nina, Teresa, Creston, and Victoria.
    —F. R.

ISBN 0-439-51275-1

Text copyright © 2002 by Jonathan London.
Illustrations copyright © 2002 by Frank Remkiewicz.
All rights reserved.
Published by Scholastic Inc., 557 Broadway, New York, NY 10012,
by arrangement with Viking Children's Books, a member of Penguin Putnam Inc.
SCHOLASTIC and associated logos are trademarks and/or registered trademarks of Scholastic Inc.

12 11 10 9 8 7 6 5 4 3 2 1   3 4 5 6 7 8/0

Printed in the U.S.A.   08

First Scholastic printing, March 2003

He flopped over to see Miss Martin,
the music teacher—*flop flop flop*.
"What's the big prize?" asked Froggy.
"It's a surprise!" she said.
"If you and your friends start a marching band,
and compete against other schools in the
Apple Blossom Parade—you can win the prize!"

"What will I play?" wondered Froggy.
Then he remembered his dad's old sax.

And after school,
he flopped up to the attic—*flop flop flop*—
and started blowing his dad's horn—
honk! bleep! screeeeeech!

FRROOGGYY!

called his dad.
"Wha–a–a t?"
"Quiet please! I'm on the phone!"

"I'm on the phone, too," cried Froggy.
"The *SAX*ophone!"—*honk!*

Next day, Froggy got his band together
and they practiced in his yard.
Max on drums—*ka-BOOM!*
Leah on triangle—*ting-a-ling!*
Emma on recorder—*tweedle-dee!*
And Hannah, her twin, on cymbals—*CLASH!*

"I want to join, too!" said Frogilina.
"What do *you* play?" asked Froggy.
"Nothing," she said. "But I can do *this*."
And she twirled a baton,
tossed it high into the air . . .

and caught it behind her back!—"Ta-*da!*"

Every day after school, Froggy's Ragtag Band
marched around and around the playground—
Honk! ka-BOOM! ting-a-ling! tweedle-dee! CLASH!

And every day, Miss Martin told them the rules for marching:
"Don't look left.
Don't look right.
And DON'T STOP FOR ANYTHING!"

"What if you have to go to the bathroom?"
asked Froggy.
"DON'T STOP FOR *ANYTHING!*"
commanded Miss Martin.
"Or everybody behind you
will crash into you!"

Three weeks left.

Two weeks.

One.

Froggy practiced marching everywhere—
even in his sleep.

At last, the big day came.
The apple trees had burst into bloom,
and the parade was ready to begin.
Everybody was nervous—
especially Froggy.

Miss Martin said, "Now remember:
    Don't look left.
    Don't look right.
    And DON'T STOP FOR ANYTHING!"
And the parade began.

Being the youngest,
    Froggy's band marched in front,
        led by the majorette—
            the one and only Frogilina.

FRROOGGYY!

called his father—
he was jumping up and down
on the sidelines.
But Froggy didn't look.

FRROOGGYY!

called his mother—
she was aiming a camera.

But Froggy didn't look.
Cameras flashed. Clowns threw candy.
And still Froggy marched, looking straight ahead.
Here came the judges' stand.
This was the big moment!

Frogilina twirled her baton.
She tossed it high into the air . . .
and Froggy thought:
        Don't look left.
        Don't look right.
        And—

BONK! Her baton hit him on the head
and knocked him down.
"Oops!" cried Froggy, looking more red
in the face than green.
Oof! Clang! Crash!—
and the rest of the parade piled on.

FRROOGGYY!

called Miss Martin.
"Wha-a-a-t?" came a muffled cry.
"Are you all right?"

Froggy crawled out
from the bottom of the heap,
and said, "DON'T STOP FOR ANYTHING!"
and started to wail a wild swamp tune
on his saxophone.

The rest of his band joined in,
and everybody danced in the street!
And when the judges' vote came in . . .
Froggy's Ragtag Band had won a *special* award:
COOLEST MARCHING BAND
AT THE APPLE BLOSSOM PARADE.

"What's the big prize?" asked Froggy.
"This is!" said Frogilina.
And she gave him a big juicy kiss
smack on his cheek—*EEEEEEEEEK!*

Then the judges gave Froggy and his band
the *real* prize—a big golden trophy
in the shape of a saxophone.

"*Yes!*" cried Froggy.
And Froggy's Ragtag Band
played one last time—
Honk! ka-BOOM! ting-a-ling! tweedle-dee! CLASH!